The Light upon Eyes

Noor & Naina

Aslam Sheik

TANEESHA
PUBLISHERS

Title : The Light Upon Eyes

Author : Aslam Sheik

Edition : First (January, 2025)

ISBN : 9789348037121

Published by

TANEESHA PUBLISHERS | *A Venture by -* **PRACHI DIGITAL PUBLICATION**

Regd. Add.: 254, Khuriyakhatta No. 10, Bindukhatta,
Lalkuan, Nainital - 262402, Uttarakhand, India
Website : www.taneeshapublishers.in
E-mail : taneeshapublishers@gmail.com
Phone : +91 8454 812712, +91 8057 812712

Printed by :
Manipal Technologies Limited, Bengaluru - 560001, Karnataka

Foreword

In a realm where the ethereal and the earthly intertwine, in the Land of Souls, this is not merely a story, it is a journey of love and longing that transcends the boundaries of life itself. Noor and Naina are not just characters; they are mirrors reflecting the depths of our own hearts, the struggles of our spirit, and the quiet beauty of finding connection in the most unexpected places.

This novel invites you to step into a world where the soul is the protagonist, where emotions flow like rivers, and where love is not limited by the physical but illuminated by the spiritual. It is a tale of two souls who meet in a land beyond our comprehension, yet whose trials and triumphs feel intimately familiar.

As you turn these pages, you will find yourself immersed in a narrative that challenges the routine and embraces the mystical. Through Noor and Naina's journey, you will question the meaning of existence, celebrate the strength of connection, and perhaps even redefine the essence of love.

This book is for anyone who has ever yearned for something beyond the tangible, who has sought solace in the unseen and who believes in the magic of the soul's journey.

Welcome to The Land of Souls. May its words touch your heart, ignite your imagination, and leave you changed.

I hope this book 'The Light upon Eyes,' brings light to your spiritual eyes as the name reflects. Ameen

The One who created the fig and painted the sky,
Who spread the earth and set the stars up high,
In His hands lies the balance, the day and the night,
The giver of wisdom, the source of all light.

He shaped the mountains, the rivers that flow,
The seed in the soil, the wind's gentle blow.
Each fig a miracle, each leaf a sign,
A sign of mercy, a design so divine.

The sky is His canvas, a palette so grand,
Each color a reminder of His mighty hand.
In the fig's sweetness, a taste of His grace,
In the vastness of the heavens, we see His embrace .

Pause and reflect, let your heart testify,
To the One who created the fig and painted the sky.

The Storyline

Chapter 1
The Land of Souls

In the endless expanse of the realm of souls, there was no concept of time. There was no morning, no dusk. No rising of the sun, no setting of it either. Here, the souls gathered in perfect stillness, suspended in a vast, featureless space. They had no names, no memories, no desires, only their essence, pure and untarnished. This was the first life of every soul: before they were sent to Earth, before they tasted human suffering, love, or joy.

Millions upon millions of souls stood in rows stretching beyond any horizon, forming an unbroken line, a sea of spirit that pulsated with quiet, meditative energy. Each soul was focused inward, not on any thought or task but on their submission to the inevitable fate that awaited them. They knew they would be sent to Earth someday. Each would take on the form of flesh and bone, living among humans, subject to the trials of life, pain, temptation, and ultimately death.

But for now, there was only peace.

Their existence was marked by a stillness that was both comforting and disorienting. There was no conversation, no movement. Silence reigned, not as a lack of sound, but as a state of being. It was the silence of submission, of knowing that their future was not theirs to decide. They waited, not with eagerness, but with an acceptance that could not be broken. There was nothing to long for, no concept of better or worse, good or evil. All of that would come later, on Earth, where their souls would be tested.

An Angel , whose form sparkled between formless light and something resembling a human figure, glided silently among them, watching over the souls. The Angel was a guardian, a guide for their journey from this peaceful existence to the world of chaos they would one day enter. It did not speak, for there was no need. The souls knew their role, and they submitted to it without question.

It had always been this way.

But then, for the first time in the infinite silence, something shifted.

Among the millions of souls, one began to stir. Its focus wavered, and a subtle ripple passed through the meditative calm. It was a small thing at first—just like a glitch, like a breeze disturbing the surface of a still lake.

But in a place where nothing had ever stirred, this disruption was immense.

The soul, soon to be known as Noor, felt something foreign within itself. A pull, a force tugging at the edges of its awareness, drawing its attention away from the silent submission that had defined its existence. It was not supposed to feel this way. Souls did not have desires, not here, not yet. But Noor could not ignore the pull. It was insistent, growing stronger, pulling him away from the line, from the others.

He turned, though turning wasn't a physical action here, there were no bodies, no limbs to move. It was more like his essence shifted, refocusing attention behind him, where the source of this disturbance lay.

And there, amidst the millions of still and silent souls, he saw it; another soul, just like one. It stood in its place like all the others, yet it was different. He could feel it. Its presence radiated a kind of energy that he had never felt before. It was curious, inquisitive. It was… reaching for him.

For the first time in its existence, Noor felt something stir inside him, something parallel to what humans might call longing or fascination. His focus on the eternal peace around him shattered and he found himself drawn toward this other soul. He wanted to get closer, to understand what this feeling was.

But such movement was not permitted here. Souls were to remain in their place, meditating in silence, waiting for their turn to be sent to Earth. No soul had ever broken the formation. Yet here he was, being pulled toward this one, unable to resist the invisible force connecting them.

This soul was different. It was… Naina, say soon to be on Earth.

He didn't know her name, not yet, but he could feel something beyond the spirit of her soul. It was as if their fates had already intertwined in a way that defied the order of things. This was no mere coincidence, no random pull. There was a reason he was drawn to her. He could feel it in the very core of his being.

But the more he focused on her, the more the peace within him failed. The longer he gazed at her, the more restless he became, as if his heart from the future has already found it's beat. What was happening to him? What was this feeling? No soul had ever felt this before. And what did it mean?

Suddenly, a blinding light filled the space between them. It was not the light of warmth or comfort, but something powerful, something divine. The Angel appeared before him, its luminous form shining with a brilliance that eclipsed the other souls. Its voice echoed through the silence, though it did not speak in words.

"You have been distracted, Noor." The sound of the Angel 's voice was not harsh, but it passed with it the weight of judgment.

Noor trembled, or would have, if his form had been capable of trembling. *"I... I don't know what happened. There was something... someone. I couldn't focus. I couldn't..."*

The Angel 's light dimmed slightly, and it floated closer, its form shifting as it spoke again. *"What you felt was desire. What you experienced was curiosity. These are human emotions. You are not meant to feel them yet, not here."*

Noor Didn't understand. What are emotions, he questioned himself. *"But why? Why did I feel it? What was it?"*

The Angel 's form flickered, its light becoming softer, as if it understood the pressure of Noor's confused state.

"The one you saw has already begun its journey. She will be sent to Earth soon, where she will face trials that you cannot comprehend. What you felt was the beginning of the bond that will be tested in the world of men. But be warned, Noor: her path is one of great difficulty. She is destined for failure, for sin. She will fall, and when she returns here, she will face judgment."

Noor recoiled at the Angel 's words. Failure? Sin? What did these words mean? He had never known the concept of good or evil before. It was foreign, and yet, something inside him rebelled against the idea that Naina was doomed.

He exploded in the form of virtual pain. *"No. I can't accept that. If her path is so dark, I want to go with her. I will save her."*

The Angel 's light flared, its form becoming larger, more imposing. *"You cannot save another soul from their fate, Noor. It is written. Each soul must face the trials of life on their own. You will be sent to Earth in time, but her path is hers alone."*

Noor was not in a state to absorb anything, he continued. *"Then I will go to Earth now. I will find her and guide her back before it's too late."* But he was not arrogant.

There was a long pause. The silence that followed was deeper than anything Noor had ever known. The other souls, still lost in their meditative state, seemed untouched by this disruption. But Noor and the Angel stood apart now, caught in a moment that felt like it would decide his entire existence.

Finally, the Angel spoke again, its voice softer now, almost sorrowful.

"If you choose this path, know that it will not be easy. You will forget all of this when you are born as a man. You will be tested by the same desires, the same weaknesses. You may not remember why you chose this path, but the bond you feel now will guide you, even in your darkest moments. But understand this, Noor: you cannot change her fate. You can only witness it."

Noor felt something like pain, a strange sensation, deep within his essence. He didn't know if it was fear or sorrow, but he knew one thing for certain: he could not stand by and do nothing.

He might have felt courage when he said, *"I accept it. I will go to Earth. I will find her."*

The Angel 's form began to fade, its light dissolving into the endless expanse of souls. *"So be it. Your journey begins."*

And with that the silence returned, but it was no longer peaceful. Noor was no longer just a soul among

millions. He was something more, something broken yet determined.

He had chosen his path and he was the first to do. He did this for love, which he will realize much later.

Chapter 2

A Forbidden Attraction

The world of souls remained as it had always been silent, ordered and peaceful. But for Noor, that tranquility had been shattered. The pull he had felt toward Naina, that brief forbidden glimpse of her soul, was like a crack in the perfect stillness of his existence. Now, every moment he spent in meditation was filled with an air of longing, a growing awareness that he could not return to the state of peaceful submission.

A forbidden attraction had taken root within him.

In the days or what felt like days, though time had no meaning here—since his encounter with the Angel, Noor had tried to push the feelings away. He tried to lose himself in the collective silence of the souls around him, but the more he attempted to focus, the more his mind drifted back to her.

There was no such thing as distance in the world of souls. Here, all souls existed in a state of unity, yet Noor felt an overwhelming sense of separation. He searched the infinite rows, looking for her, hoping to catch another glimpse, but Naina was gone. The Angel had said her time had come to be sent to Earth and with her departure a deep void was left in her place.

Still, the sensation lingered. It was as though a piece of her remained with him, a thread that bound them together across the vast space between their worlds. This connection was not supposed to exist. Souls were meant to be free from desire, free from the entanglements of earthly emotions. But Noor could no longer deny it: he wanted to be near her.

For the first time, he felt an ache within his being, a longing that defied the very nature of his existence. It was unlike anything he had ever known, and with it came a dawning realization: this was love. Not the fleeting, imperfect love of humans, but something deeper, more profound—**a love that transcended time and space. It was not born from familiarity or shared experiences, but from a fundamental recognition, a pull toward something that was already part of him.**

Yet, it was forbidden. Here.

The Angel stood tall, radiant with divine light that danced like liquid gold. The souls gathered, glowing softly in hues of ethereal white and silver, forming a vast ocean of energy. Silence fell as the angel began to speak, each word resonating with the weight of truth.

"O luminous creations, bearers of life and witnesses of eternity, your existence is no accident, nor are you mere fragments in the wind. You are the breath of the Divine endowed with meaning and destiny. Placed into clay, given form and entrusted with purpose.

Know this: you were not created aimlessly. Life and death are but veils through which your true essence is revealed. Every deed, every thought, every choice is a brushstroke on the canvas of your soul.

Reflect on this truth: life is but a passage, not a destination. Your purpose lies not in what you own, but in who you become. Your worth is not in worldly gains, but in the purity of your soul.

You carry the trust of free will—an honor and a responsibility. You were created to choose, to strive, and to seek the One who created you. Every heartbeat, every breath, is a question: Who will you serve? Your Master? Or your temptations?.

Your life is not a coincidence; it is guided by a wisdom that knows no bounds. Trust the path, even when it feels uncertain, for He leads you through the unseen.

You carry within you the light of judgement. It whispers in moments of doubt, nudging you toward truth. Listen, for your choices shape not only your world but your eternity.

But do not confine worship to rituals alone. Worship is to align your will with His. It is to love, to give, to forgive. To seek knowledge and act with justice. To serve humanity as you serve Him.

O souls, you are born to seek, to love, to transcend. Your purpose is not bound by time but stretches into eternity.

You are not alone. Your bonds with others are threads in the fabric of existence. Love, honor, and forgive, for in doing so, you mirror the mercy of your Creator.

Your lives are intertwined, your trials shared. The stranger you meet, the enemy you face, even those who wound you—each is a test, a teacher, sent to guide your soul toward Him. Be patient, for patience is the key to understanding.

Know that every deed matters. Every smile, every kind word, every act of humility echoes across the unseen realms. Nothing is lost, for the scales of justice are perfect.

Do not cling to the fleeting. Your next stop, the Earth is but a mirage, a shadow. What lies beyond is eternal, vast, and incomprehensible in its beauty. Prepare for it, for the journey does not end there.

When the path grows dark, and your burden heavy, remember: your Lord sees, and He is near. Every wound will heal, every tear will be counted, every loss restored. Trust in His wisdom, for He writes your story with love.

When the storms of life rage within you, turn to Him. His remembrance is your anchor, His love your sanctuary.

The power to rise, to transform, lies within you. Your will is your compass, your intentions the seeds of your destiny. Tend them well, for the harvest will be eternal.

Your titles, wealth, and lineage mean nothing in the realm of souls. It is your piety, your sincerity that defines you. Strive for consciousness, the consciousness of your Creator in every moment.

Chase not the fleeting illusions of this world. Your true home lies beyond, in gardens where rivers flow and sorrow is but a forgotten dream.

Prepare for this garden with deeds that echo mercy, kindness, and justice. Your Creator has promised, and His promise is truth.

Humility is your crown. Walk with it, for it is in lowering yourself before the Creator that you ascend. Greatness lies not in power but in surrender.

You are guardians of creation, entrusted with care, not dominion. The Earth whispers His name in every tree, river and sky. Honor it, for it is your sanctuary and your test.

O souls, return to your Lord with humility and hope. Seek Him in the beauty of creation, in the love you give and receive, in the silence of prayer, and the courage to rise after every fall. Your journey is not without meaning. It is an invitation to know Him, to love Him, and ultimately, to return to Him.

Carry these truths with you as you enter the realm of existence. Shine with the light of faith, and let your actions leave a legacy of goodness. For every soul gathered here today will one day stand before Him, and on that Day, nothing will matter but the purity of your heart."

The angel's light expanded, bathing the souls in radiance. The air was heavy with meaning, as though every word carried the weight of eternity. And it reminded once again;

"O luminous ones, when you descend into the world, carry this wisdom in your hearts. Let it guide you in every breath, every step, and every moment of doubt. For soon, you will return, and your soul will carry the weight of what you have sown."

"Go forth, O souls, and fulfill your trust with wisdom and grace. Eternity awaits."

The Angel's voice faded leaving behind a profound silence. The souls, once unformed and restless, now glowed with purpose, their essence vibrating with divine understanding as they prepared to descend into existence.

As the other souls remained lost in their serene meditation, Noor's thoughts raced. He wondered what she was experiencing on Earth. Was she frightened? Was she alone? The Angel had warned that she was destined for failure, that her path would lead her into darkness. But Noor couldn't accept that. He believed, deep down, that there was a way to save her, a way to change her fate. And if there was, he would find it.

But as these thoughts grew more intense, so too did the choice of his own responsibility. He once had chosen to remain in this realm of souls, safe from the trials of Earth, free from the corruption of the physical world. And yet, here he was, plagued by desires he was not meant to feel.

It was clear now that Naina's presence had awakened something within him. It wasn't just about her; it was about what she represented, a gateway to understanding human experience, to knowing love, pain, and sacrifice. And with that understanding came another choice.

He could stay in this land, untouched by the turmoil of Earth, or he could follow her.

In a moment of unspoken thought, Noor called out, not with words, but with his essence. He reached for the guardian Angel, who had appeared to him before. There were no voices here, no language, but the Angel understood the silent plea, and once again, its brilliant form appeared before him.

The Angel's presence brought a sense of gravity, a reminder of the divine order that governed all things. Its light dimmed slightly as it addressed Noor. *"You are troubled, Noor."*

Noor did not hesitate. He could not afford to. *"I cannot let her go. I need to find her, to protect her."*

The Angel's form flickered, as if contemplating the emotion of his words. *"You were warned. She has gone to Earth, and her path is one of darkness. You cannot save her from the fate that awaits her. I ask you once again, Are you Su..... "*

Before the Angel finished, Noor interrupted. *"Then send me to her. If she is destined to fall, let me fall with her. I would rather face the trials of Earth than remain here, knowing she is lost."*

Noor could feel the intensity of the Angel's gaze on him, though the Angel had no eyes in the way humans did. It seemed to search him, to weigh his determination against the cost of the decision he was about to make.

Angel then said, *"You do not understand what you ask for. Earth is a place of suffering, of temptation. Even now, you are not immune to the desires that plague humanity. If you go to Earth, you will face those trials—hunger, lust, pride, greed. The things you feel now are only a shadow of what you will experience in the physical world."*

Noor hesitated, but only for a moment. The Angel's words echoed in his mind, but they did not deter him. He had already made his choice. *"I understand the risk. But I cannot stay here and do nothing. I need to find her. I need to try."*

The Angel's light flared, and for a brief moment, it was as if the entire realm of souls was illuminated by its radiance. When the light dimmed again, the Angel's voice was softer, more measured. *"You are not the first soul to make this choice. Many have sought to change the fate of another, to defy the will of the Creator. Most are consumed by the very darkness they sought to overcome."*

Noor's determination wavered for only an instant, but the feeling passed. He had come too far to turn back now. *"I will face whatever I must. Just send me to her."* But once again he was not arrogant when he asked for this.

The Angel paused, and when it spoke again, there was a note of resignation in its voice. *"Very well. But know this, Noor, once you enter the world of men, you will forget this conversation. You will forget the purpose that drives you. You will forget her. All you will have is the faint memory of a promise, a bond that you will not fully understand. And when the time comes, you will be tested. The question is not whether you will find her, but whether you will remember why."*

Noor bowed his head, a gesture that felt strange in a realm where he had no body, but it was the only way he knew to convey his acceptance. *"I accept."*

The Angel's light began to recede, and Noor could feel the boundaries of the realm of souls dissolving around him. The peace that had once defined his existence was slipping away, replaced by a growing sense of anticipation, of fear and of purpose.

Noor's essence began to unravel, as if he were being pulled apart by invisible threads. The sensation was unlike anything he had ever known—disorienting, terrifying, but also strangely exhilarating. For the first time, he understood what it meant to be mortal. He could feel himself being drawn down, down into the physical realm, where his soul would be bound to flesh and bone, where he would face the trials of humanity.

As his awareness faded, the last thing he saw was the Angel, watching over him, its light growing dimmer as he descended into the world of men.

And then there was darkness as the Angel said. "Go, then. Your journey begins."

The transition was not immediate. It was not a simple falling from one realm into another. Rather, it was a slow unravelling, as if Noor's soul was being pulled apart thread by thread, each piece of him slowly dissolving into the ether. It was not painful, but it was disorienting, a sensation of losing oneself, of forgetting everything that had ever been certain.

Noor tried to hold on to the memory of Naina, the feeling of her presence, but even that began to slip away. The Angel had warned him that this would happen but knowing it did not make the experience any easier. He could feel the peace of the soul's realm fading, replaced by something far more chaotic, far more unpredictable.

For a brief moment, Noor was suspended between worlds, neither soul nor man, caught in a neutral space where time had no meaning. He could feel the stress of his choice pressing down on his chest, the enormity of what he had agreed to.

And then, with a sudden rush of sensation, it was over.

Chapter 3

On Earth: The Awakening

Noor opened his eyes, gasping for breath, though he did not yet know what breath was. His body, his new human body was trembling, his heart beating faster as he struggled to make sense of the sensations flooding his mind. The ground beneath him was rough and cold, the air thick with smells and sounds that overwhelmed his senses.

He sat up slowly, his limbs weak and unsteady. He did not know where he was, only that he was alone. The memories of his life as a soul were gone, replaced by a deep, aching confusion. But somewhere, deep within him, a voice whispered a name, a name that would guide him on his journey.

Naina.

He did not know who she was, or why her name echoed in his mind, but he knew one thing for certain: he had to find her.

The world was vast and full of dangers, but Noor was no longer the peaceful, serene soul he had once been. He was a man now, and his journey had only just begun.

His body was shaking upright as if pulled from the depths of a dream. His breath came in short, ragged gasps, and for a moment, he didn't know where he was. The world around him was blurry, the colors too bright, the sounds too sharp. He blinked, trying to make sense of it all.

He was lying on the ground, the rough texture of dirt and grass beneath his hands. The air was thick and humid, filled with the scent of earth and something else, something he couldn't quite place. His body felt strange, foreign, as if it didn't quite belong to him. His limbs were heavy, and his heart pounded in his chest, each beat a reminder of his new, fragile existence.

Slowly, he pushed himself to his feet, his legs shaking beneath him. He was unsteady, as if he had never stood before, and perhaps he hadn't. This body was new to him, a vessel that he had only just inhabited.

He looked around, taking in his surroundings. He was in a forest, the trees towering above him, their branches swaying gently in the breeze. The sunlight filtered through the leaves, casting spotted shadows on the ground. It was beautiful, but also overwhelming. The world was too bright, too loud, too alive. He had never experienced anything like it before.

And then, slowly, the memories began to fade.

The peace of the soul's realm, the Angel's warnings, even the feeling of Naina's presence, all of it slipped away, like water through his fingers. He tried to hold on to it, tried to remember why he had come here, but it was no use. The memories were gone, leaving only a vague sense of purpose, a feeling that there was something he needed to do, someone he needed to find.

But who? And why?

Noor's became restless as the questions flooded his mind, but no answers came. He was alone, lost in a world he didn't understand, with no memory of who he was or why he had been sent here.

But even in his confusion, there was a sense of determination, a quiet resolve that guided his steps as he began to walk through the forest. He didn't know where he was going, but he knew that he had to keep moving. There was someone out there, someone he was meant to find. And somehow, someway, he would find her.

As Noor wandered through the unfamiliar world, the result of his choice began to settle on him. He didn't understand it fully yet, but deep within him, there was a knowledge that this life, this fragile, fleeting existence, was the result of a decision he had made long ago. A decision that had bound him to the world of men, to the trials and temptations that awaited him.

The Angel had warned him of the dangers, of the difficulties he would face. And now, as he stumbled through the forest, unsure of his place in this world, Noor began to understand just how difficult his path would be.

But despite the fear, despite the uncertainty, there was something else within him, something that kept him moving forward.

Hope.

Even in the midst of his confusion, even as the memories of his previous existence faded, Noor held on to that hope. It was fragile, yes, but it was enough. Enough to keep him going. Enough to keep him searching.

For what, he didn't yet know.

But he would find it.

Noor is now reborn as a man, grown and lost in the chaos of Earth..

"I am waiting for something... someone... but what? Why does this longing tear at my insides like a wound that will never heal?" he asked himself.

The sun hung low in the sky, casting long shadows across the landscape. Noor had been walking for what felt like hours, though he couldn't be sure. Time was a strange concept to him now, something he was still getting used to. In the realm of souls, there had been no time, only an eternal present. But here, on

Earth, everything was measured. Moments slipped away, irretrievable, like sand falling through an hourglass.

Each step Noor took was a reminder of his new body, his new existence getting closer to his end. Every sensation was unfamiliar, overwhelming in its intensity. The air felt heavy against his skin, the ground rough beneath his feet. His muscles ached from the effort of walking, and his throat was dry, parched from thirst. He had never felt thirst before. It was a strange, gnawing sensation that made him long for something he couldn't yet identify.

Noor's breath came in ragged gasps as he reached the top of a small hill. Below him, the forest stretched out endlessly, a sea of green and brown. The sky above was splashed with pink and gold, the last light of day fading into dusk. He stood there for a moment, looking out at the world, trying to make sense of it all.

The memories of the soul's realm were slipping away, dissolving like mist in the morning sun. He could no longer remember the peace he had once felt, the stillness that had defined his existence. All that remained was a vague sense of purpose, an echo of something important that he had forgotten.

As night began to fall, Noor found shelter beneath a large oak tree. He sat down, leaning against the rough rock and closed his eyes. His body ached, and he was exhausted in a way he had never known before. The fatigue of a human body was nothing like the calm repose of a soul. It was intense, oppressive and inescapable.

But as he rested, a new sensation began to stir within him, something deeper than the physical discomfort he was experiencing. It was an emotion, raw and unfiltered, unlike anything he had ever felt before. It started as a small knot in his chest, but it grew, expanding until it filled his entire being.

Loneliness.

In the realm of souls, there had been no such thing as loneliness. All souls existed in perfect harmony, connected by the divine presence that bound them together. But here, in this human world, Noor felt utterly and completely alone. The vastness of the Earth stretched out before him, and yet, he was isolated, cut off from everything he had once known.

He longed for something, though he didn't know what. Connection, perhaps or understanding. Or maybe it was Naina, this mysterious presence that seemed to call to him from the depths of his soul. He didn't know her, but he felt as though she were the only one who could ease the ache inside him.

For the first time, Noor felt confused of his choice. He had given up the peace of the souls' realm, the certainty of divine purpose, for this—this chaotic, unpredictable existence. And yet, despite the fear and confusion, there was something else within him, something that pushed him forward.

Hope. Now with purpose.

Even in the dark of his loneliness, there was a light of hope. A belief that he was here for a reason, that his journey had a purpose. He just had to find it.

That night, as Noor drifted into a fitful sleep, he experienced his first dream. In the realm of souls, there had been no dreams, no subconscious, no need for the mind to sort through emotions and experiences. But here, in this human body, his mind was alive, teeming with images and feelings that he didn't fully understand.

The dream began in darkness, a void that stretched out endlessly. Noor floated through the void, weightless, searching for something he couldn't name. He could feel it, a presence, a light, just beyond his reach. He moved toward it, driven by a deep unshakable need.

And then, out of the darkness, she appeared.

Naina.

She stood before him, her figure glowing with a soft, golden light. Her face was obscured, but he could feel her, her essence, her soul. It was the same presence he had felt in the realm of souls, the same pull that had drawn him to her in the first place.

But as Noor reached out to her, the light began to fade. Her form flickered, growing dimmer and dimmer, until she was nothing more than a shadow. Noor called out to her, his voice echoing in the void, but she was gone.

He was alone again.

Noor woke up with a jerk, his heart pounding in his chest. The dream lingered in his mind, vivid and haunting. It had felt so real, so tangible, as if Naina had been right there with him. But now, in the cold light of dawn, he was once again faced with the reality of his situation.

He was alone.

But the dream had left him with a sense of clarity. He knew now, without a doubt, that Naina was the key to his journey. She was the reason he had come to Earth, the reason he had given up everything. He just didn't know why.

As the days passed, Noor's understanding of his new human form grew. He learned to navigate the physical world, though it was often a struggle. His muscles ached from the constant exertion, and his senses were bombarding that overwhelmed him.

But there was also a strange beauty in it all. The feel of the wind against his skin, the sound of leaves rustling in the trees, the taste of fresh water on his tongue, these were experiences he had never known as a soul, and though they were unfamiliar, they were also wondrous in their own way.

Noor marveled at the complexity of the human body, the way it could feel pain and pleasure in equal measure. There was a fragility to it, yes, but also a resilience. The human body can endure, adapt, and survive. And Noor was beginning to understand that survival was a key part of human experience.

But the greatest challenge for Noor was not the physical world, it was the emotional and spiritual journey he was on. He had been sent to Earth with a purpose, but that purpose was shrouded in mystery. And his understanding of who he truly was.

There were moments when Noor felt lost, adrift in a world that made no sense to him. But in those moments, he would remember the dream, the image of Naina, glowing in the darkness. It was the one thing that grounded him, the one thing that gave him direction.

And slowly, as the days turned into weeks, Noor began to awaken to something deeper within himself. A connection to the divine, a thread that still tied him to the realm of souls, even though he could no longer fully remember it. He could feel it in the quiet moments, in the stillness of the forest, in the way the sunlight filtered through the trees.

It was a reminder that he was not truly alone. The divine presence was still with him, guiding him, even though he couldn't fully understand it. And with that realization came a sense of peace, a small taste of the calmness he had once known in the realm of souls.

But the peace was fleeting, always overshadowed by the growing sense of urgency. Time was moving, slipping away and Noor knew that he couldn't remain in this forest forever. He had a journey to complete, a person to find.

Chapter 4

The Mountain Dream

Noor had recurring dreams of a distant mountain with a goat tied to a hut, symbolic of his quest. He ignored the dreams at first, dismissing them as mere nightmares, until the Angel reappeared in his dreams to remind him of his task. Guiding him on the path and to begin the journey to find Naina.

Noor: *"I cannot find someone I don't even remember."*

Angel: *"You will remember her when the time comes. Until then, your path is to walk in faith."*

Noor had been walking for days. His body, once foreign and difficult to control, was now becoming familiar, though it still felt strange to him. The weight of it, the limitations, the constant need for food and water, it all wore on him. Each step felt heavier than the last, his muscles protesting with every movement. But still, he pushed forward, driven by something deep within him, something he couldn't fully explain.

The air around him was growing colder, the dense forest thinning as he began to ascend into the foothills of a mountain range. The trees stood tall and ancient, their crooked roots twisting through the earth like the veins of the land itself. A cold wind whipped through the valley, biting at his skin but Noor barely noticed. His mind was elsewhere, consumed by the image of Naina that had haunted his dreams since the moment he had arrived on Earth.

He had no map, no destination, but he felt that the mountain held something for him, an answer perhaps, or a vision. There was a pull, a subtle tug that guided him forward, urging him to keep going despite the exhaustion that weighed on his limbs.

As night fell, Noor found himself at the base of a great mountain. Its pointed peak rose high above him, disappearing into the clouds. The sight of it filled him with both awe and a strange sense of foreboding. It was majestic and ancient, yet there was something in its shadow that made him uneasy, as if the mountain itself held secrets that he wasn't ready to uncover.

With no shelter in sight, Noor found a small hollow in the side of the mountain, where the rock extended out just enough to provide some protection from the wind. Exhausted, he curled up beneath the overhang, pulling his thin coat tighter around him which he found in the forest last night. Sleep came quickly and with it the dream.

In his dream, Noor stood at the foot of the mountain once more, but the landscape was different, stranger, more surreal. The sky above was a deep, swirling purple, with stars that twinkled too brightly, casting an eerie glow over the land. The air was thick with the scent of something ancient, something powerful and it filled his lungs with a sense of both dread and wonder.

He looked up and the mountain loomed before him, larger and more imposing than it had been in the real world. The peak seemed impossibly high, stretching into the heavens, and Noor knew without a doubt that he had to climb it.

He began to ascend, his movements slow and deliberate. The path was steep, the rocks sharp beneath his feet, but there was no pain. He felt weightless, as if his body had been left behind and only his soul remained to make the climb. The higher he went, the more the world around him began to shift and change. The ground beneath him crumbled, turning to dust with each step, but he kept moving, drawn upward by a force he couldn't see.

As he climbed, he began to hear whispers, soft at first but growing louder with each step. The voices were indistinct but they filled his mind, echoing through the corridors of his consciousness. They spoke of choices, of fate, of love and loss. Noor couldn't make out the words, but he felt their meaning deep within him, resonating in his very core.

The path grew steeper and soon he was scrambling up the rocks, his hands grasping for more as the ground shifted beneath him. The mountain seemed to be alive, moving and breathing with every step he took. The whispers grew louder, more insistent, until they were a deafening roar in his ears.

And then, suddenly, the path levelled out.

Noor found himself standing on a narrow ledge, the peak of the mountain still far above him. Before him, a great abyss yawned open, its depths lost in shadow. The air here was colder, thinner, and it made his head swim. He felt unsteady, as if the very ground beneath him might give way at any moment.

Across the abyss, on the other side of the ledge, stood a figure.

It was Naina.

She was standing there, just as she had in his earlier dreams, her form glowing with a soft, ethereal light. Her face was still obscured, but he could feel her presence, strong and undeniable. She was so close, yet so far, separated from him by the vast abyss that stretched between them.

Noor's heart dived in his chest. He took a step forward, his hands reaching out toward her, but the ground beneath him trembled and he froze. The space was wide and deep, and there was no way to cross it. He looked around, desperate for some way to reach her, but there was none.

Naina stood still, her gaze fixed on him, though her eyes remained hidden in shadow. She said nothing, but her silence was heavy, filled with unspoken words, with questions and answers he couldn't yet grasp. Noor felt a surge of frustration, of helplessness. He was so close, but it wasn't enough. He needed to reach her. He needed to understand why she was here, why she haunted his dreams, why he felt this unbreakable bond with her.

But no matter how hard he tried, he couldn't cross the abyss.

The mountain seemed to mock him, its pointed edges looming around him, the whispers growing louder once more. They swirled around him, filling his mind with doubt, with fear. Was this his fate? To be forever separated from her, to chase her through dreams and never find her.

Noor looked down into the abyss, its depths pulling at him, tempting him to leap, to fall. The darkness was comforting in a strange way, offering an end to the struggle, a release from the constant search. He could feel it calling to him, urging him to let go, to give in.

But then, out of the silence, he heard her voice.

"Noor…… Don't fall, Noor."

Her voice was soft, but it cut through the noise, through the chaos, anchoring him to the moment. He looked up and for the first time, he saw her eyes, dark and deep, filled with both sorrow and hope. Her gaze held him and in that instant he knew, he couldn't fall, he couldn't give in.

He had to climb higher.

With a renewed sense of determination, Noor turned away from the chasm. The path up the mountain was steep and treacherous, but he didn't hesitate. He began to climb once more, his hands gripping the rough stone, his feet finding purchase on the jagged rocks. The whispers faded, replaced by the sound of his own breath, steady and sure.

Naina's presence lingered behind him, watching, waiting but she said nothing more. Noor didn't need her to speak. He could feel her with him, guiding him, urging him onward.

After what felt like an eternity, Noor reached the summit of the mountain. The air was thin and his body ached, but he had made it. He stood at the peak, looking out over the world below. The view was breathtaking, endless forests, rivers and valleys stretching out beneath him, bathed in the soft glow of twilight.

But there, at the highest point, was something unexpected: a mirror.

It was tall, ancient, its frame made of twisted branches and vines. The glass was foggy, but as Noor approached, it cleared, revealing his reflection.

Or rather, what was left of him.

His reflection showed a figure that was not quite human, not quite soul. His body was translucent, fading at the edges, as if he were caught between worlds. His eyes, once filled with determination, now reflected uncertainty, fear and a growing sense of loss.

But there was something else in the mirror too.

Behind him, in the reflection, stood Naina. She was closer now, her hand resting gently on his shoulder, her face still hidden, but her presence undeniable. Her touch was light, almost invisible, but it grounded him, reminding him of why he was here.

Noor reached up to touch her hand, but as soon as he did, the mirror shattered, the glass exploding into a thousand tiny pieces that fell around him like snow.

He was alone again.

Noor wake up with a haunting thirst, his heart bleeding in loneliness. The mountain, the mirror, Naina, it had all been a dream, but it felt so real, so vivid. He could still feel the gentle touch of her hand on his shoulder, the pull of the abyss beneath him.

He sat up, blinking in the early morning light. The mountain loomed above him, unchanged, but something within him had shifted. The dream had given him something, an answer perhaps, or a glimpse of the future. He wasn't sure yet, but he knew that his journey was far from over.

The mountain had shown him the path ahead, the challenges he would face, the choices.

Chapter 5
The Market

Priest: *"You speak as though you've touched divinity, yet you walk among us as a man. Who are you?"*

Noor: *"I am no more than you. We are both lost. But I seek not to save others, only one soul."*

As Noor begins his journey, he met people from all walks of life. A priest who clings to religious doctrine but has lost his faith in people and a slum dweller who worships Noor, thinking him of a divine being. Through such encounters, Noor realized the complexity of the human soul and the trials that await Naina.

Earlier, as the sun climbed higher into the sky, Noor descended from the foothills, leaving behind the shadow of the mountain that had haunted his dreams. The world below, far removed from the silence and solitude of the peak, was alive with noise and motion. Villages dotted the landscape, their narrow streets filled with people going about their daily lives, some hurried, some at ease, all of them caught in the dance of existence that Noor was only beginning to understand.

For the first time since he had taken human form, Noor felt a strange pull towards these people. Their energy, their laughter, their pain, it was all physical, like the hum of a great machine constantly in motion. There was something raw and beautiful in the way they lived, even in their struggle. He wasn't sure why, but he felt compelled to walk among them, to witness their lives, and perhaps learn something of his own purpose through their experiences.

Noor's feet carried him to a small marketplace in a village nestled at the edge of the valley. It was a bustling place, full of color and noise. Vendors called out to passersby, selling their goods; fruits, vegetables, spices, fabrics and jewelries. The air was filled with the scent of freshly baked bread, mingling with the sharp tang of herbs and the sweet fragrance of flowers.

As he walked through the market, Noor felt a sense of awe and confusion. Everything was so vivid, so alive. He had never seen anything like this in the realm of souls, where existence had been peaceful and unchanging. Here, there was movement, chaos and emotion everywhere he looked.

He watched as people haggled over prices, their voices rising in frustration or laughter. A mother scolded her child for wandering too far, her face a mixture of fear and relief when she caught him. A young couple held hands as they walked past, their eyes shining with the light of new love. There was a vibrancy in these people, a fire that burned brightly despite the hardships they faced.

Noor found himself drawn to a small stall where an old woman sat behind a table covered in books. The sight of the books made his heart clench. He had never touched one, had never dared to in his very short life before this. His own past was still a blur, but he knew that in some way, books had once terrified him.

The old woman noticed him staring and smiled. *"Do you like to read, young man?"*

Noor hesitated. The question caught him off guard. He didn't know how to explain that he couldn't read, that the words on the pages meant nothing to him. But something in the woman's kind eyes made him want to stay. *"I... don't know how."*

The old woman's smile didn't falter. She reached for a small, worn book from the pile and held it out to him. *"It's never too late to learn. This one is about love, if that's something you're curious about."*

Noor looked at the book in her hands, but he didn't take it. Instead, he felt a surge of emotion, something that surrounded him, deep and painful. **Love**. He had no memory of it, but the word itself was heavy, as if it was a key to something lost inside him.

He whispered in a very confused and low voice. *"I don't understand it."*

The old woman chuckled softly, her eyes wrinkling at the corners. *"That's the funny thing about love. Most of us don't understand it either. But it's the trying, the search for meaning, that makes it beautiful."*

Noor thanked her quietly and moved on, though her words stayed with him. As he walked away from the market, he couldn't help but think about love, what it was, and why it seemed so important to humans. And why, in the depths of his soul, it felt like the answer to everything he was searching for.

Later that evening, Noor found himself in a small tavern at the edge of the village. The room was dimly lit, filled with the hum of conversation and the clatter of dishes. He sat alone at a corner table, watching the people around him.

Two men at the bar were deep in conversation, their voices low but intense. Noor couldn't hear the words, but he could see the tension in their bodies, the way their hands curled into fists, the way their eyes turned red with anger. Conflict. He had seen glimpses of it before, in the market, but this was different. This was personal, raw.

As their argument escalated, one of the men slammed his fist on the table, spilling his drink. The other stood abruptly, his face flushed with rage.

Man 1: *"You're a coward! You've always been a coward!"*

Man 2: *"And you've always been a fool!"*

Before Noor could react, the two men lunged at each other, fists flying. The tavern erupted in chaos as tables were overturned and people scrambled to get out of the way.

Noor felt a rush of emotions, fear, confusion, anger. He had never experienced anything like this before. In the realm of souls, there had been no conflict, no violence. Everything had been calm, harmonious. But here, in the human world, people fought. They hurt each other easily and sometimes for no reason.

He wanted to intervene, to stop the violence, but he didn't know how. His body felt heavy, frozen in place. And then, just as suddenly as it had begun, the fight was over. The tavern keeper and a few other men pulled the two combatants apart, dragging them outside into the cool night air.

Noor sat there, feeling discomfort in his chest. He felt sick, not just from the fight, but from what it represented. Conflict, pain, anger, these were all part of the human experience. And yet, despite the violence, there had been something else in the men's eyes. Something deeper, more complex. Love, maybe, or regret. A desire to be understood.

He realized then that being human was not just about experiencing joy or beauty. It was also about confronting the darkness within, the things that tore people apart. He hadn't expected that. He had thought the journey would be simpler, more straightforward. But humanity, it seemed, was full of contradictions.

Later same night, as Noor wandered the quiet streets of the village, he heard the soft sound of footsteps behind him. He turned to see a small child, no more than six or seven years old, standing a few feet away, her eyes wide with curiosity.

"Are you lost?" Her voice was sweet and innocent, and for a moment, Noor didn't know how to respond. Was he lost? In many ways, yes. He was lost in this world, lost in his own mind, trying to make sense of who he was and why he had come here.

But he didn't say that. Instead, he smiled and knelt down so he was at eye level with the girl.

"A little. But I think I'm finding my way." He wasn't sure when he said that and he realized soon that he wasn't lying. And for the very first time he liked an interaction.

The girl smiled back, her face lighting up with joy. *"My mama says that when people are lost, it means they're looking for something important. Are you looking for something?"*

Noor felt a lump form in his throat. This child, so innocent, so pure, seemed to understand more about life than he did. He didn't know how to answer her question, but he didn't have to. She took his hand and led him down the street, her small fingers warm and soft against his.

As they walked, Noor felt a sense of peace wash over him. The child's innocence, her simple joy, reminded him of something he had lost long ago. There was beauty in this world, even in the midst of pain and confusion. And maybe, just maybe, there was hope.

That night, as Noor lay beneath the stars, he thought about everything he had seen and felt that day. The market, the fight, the child, they were all pieces of the puzzle that was humanity. And yet, he still didn't have the answers he was looking for. He didn't know how his purpose was created, or why he had been drawn to this world.

But he was beginning to understand that being human wasn't about having all the answers. It was about the journey, the search for meaning, the connections people made along the way. It was about love, yes, but also about pain, conflict and forgiveness.

Noor felt the pressure of his human form, the exhaustion that came with it, but there was something else too, a quiet sense of belonging. He was a part of this world now, for better or worse. And maybe, through his encounters with humanity, he would find the answers he sought.

But for now, he would rest.

Tomorrow was another day and the journey was far from over.

Chapter 6

Temptations of The Earth

Noor: *"This body... these desires, I cannot bear them. I am not strong enough."*

Angel: *"Strength is not given, it is found. You must survive if you are to find her."*

Noor now is tested by human desires, greed, envy, and pride. He found himself drawn into the same traps that he was warned about. He faced moments where he nearly abandoned his mission, overwhelmed by the weight of human existence. The Angel intervened during his darkest moments, offering strength but not solutions.

Earlier, as Noor continued his journey through the world of humanity, he began to feel the comfort of his body more acutely. The once alien sensation of flesh and bone had become familiar and with that familiarity came a growing awareness of the pleasures and desires that surrounded him. The physical world, with its intense sensations and vivid experiences, pulled at him in ways he hadn't expected.

The village at the base of the mountain had offered him a glimpse into human life, their struggles, their love, their conflicts. But it wasn't until he ventured further into the bustling city that he encountered the true depth of earthly temptations.

The city was a living, breathing organism, its streets pulsed with life, its buildings towering like monuments to human ambition. Everywhere Noor looked, there were signs of wealth, power and indulgence. Bright lights flickered from storefronts, advertising everything from fine clothes to exotic foods, to experiences that promised pleasure beyond imagination. The air was filled with the smell of perfume, smoke and sweat, mingling into an intoxicating blend that made his senses buzz.

Here, in this city, the rules were different. People moved quickly, their eyes focused on their own pursuits, their minds filled with ambition, greed and desire. Noor felt it all, the rush of life, the pull of the material world. It was exhilarating, intoxicating even, but it was also dangerous.

He could feel the temptation growing stronger with each step he took.

Noor's first encounter with temptation came in the form of a man named Rishi. Dressed in fine clothes, with a smile that could charm anyone, Rishi was the embodiment of earthly success. He had wealth, power and influence, and he wore them like armor.

Rishi approached Noor in a crowded marketplace, his eyes gleaming with curiosity. *"You look like someone who's just arrived. New to the city?"*

Noor nodded, unsure of what to say. He was new to everything, the city, the world, the very concept of being human.

Rishi's grin widened. *"Let me show you around. This city is full of wonders. Anything you want, you can have it here."*

Noor hesitated. There was something about Rishi that made him uneasy, but there was also a pull, a magnetic attraction to the idea of having everything at his fingertips.

Before he knew it, he was following Rishi through the winding streets of the city. They passed lavish restaurants, where the scent of roasted meats and rich spices made Noor's stomach growl. They passed shops filled with luxurious clothes and jewels that sparkled under the lights. Everywhere, there was something to tempt the senses, something to make him forget the higher purpose that had once seemed so clear.

Rishi led him to an opulent bar, that was filled with the scent of incense and the low murmur of voices. Inside, people lounged on velvet cushions, sipping from delicate glasses filled with amber liquid. Noor felt out of place, but at the same time, he couldn't deny the allure of it all.

Rishi handed him a glass, filled with a drink that shimmered in the dim light. *"Drink. Relax. This is the*

way of the world. You've been too serious, too focused on things that don't matter. Here, you can let go."

Noor stared at the glass. The temptation was overwhelming. For the first time, he wondered what it would be like to give in, to indulge in the pleasures of the world, to let go of the burden of his journey. The drink sparkled invitingly, the scent of it intoxicating.

But just as he was about to take a sip, a voice echoed in his mind. A soft, familiar voice. Naina's voice. *"Don't lose yourself, Noor Remember why you're here."*

His hand trembled, and he set the glass down. *"No, I can't."*

Rishi's smile faded, just for a moment, before he leaned forward. *"Suit yourself. But remember, the world doesn't wait for those who hesitate. If you want something, you have to take it."*

Noor couldn't figure out if he really wanted it, but he sensed Rishi was very convincing. As the guilt passed his throat, he decided to question rishi on his choice. "Would you like to hurt your own mother or daughter."

Rishi wasn't expecting this and with complete surprise he expressed sharply *" What?. No... No, not at all. Why do you ask this ?*

Noor did not stop, *" Would you like to hurt someone else's mother or children?"*

Rishi kept his glass on the table, quieter now and submissive to understand where this was going and what makes him ask such things. *" No, I don't think I am that evil to do such things to anyone."*

Noor knew Rishi was ready to listen and he continued.

" A man is a protector, a provider, a caretaker, a guardian. This is not even his purpose, it's his basic role to play.

And when you consume alcohol, you chose to be intoxicated, you chose to lose your senses. You decided not to be a protector anymore, even if it seems only for a while, but without you knowing it, it already flows in your veins, veins of your future self.

You, a man, who is supposed to be a guiding light for women and children have now become a predator, hunting down his own kinds, his own responsibilities, his own purpose.

You have now become an animal and you chose to be this version of yourself, for mere pleasure, without realizing the value of being sent down to Earth, value of a human life.

Rishi, this glass of drink, that you offered me as a relaxation, is a source of all evils. You have not come here to relax, you are here to find your purpose, act upon it and find a way back.

Quit.., quit to be disgusting, quit before it's too late."

Noor stood up and rushed out of the haven, as Rishi was still in shock, not realizing how he should react, with his senses still not in his full control.

As the night wore on, Noor wandered the streets alone, the echo of Rishi's words lingering in his mind. The city was quieter now, the streets less crowded, but the temptations were still there, waiting for him at every corner.

That was when he met a woman.

She stood beneath the dim light of a streetlamp, her dark hair falling in waves over her shoulders. Her eyes, glowing like embers, locked onto the moment he saw her. She was beautiful, more beautiful than anyone Noor had ever seen yet, her presence was like a fire that drew him in.

She approached him slowly, her steps deliberate, her gaze never leaving his. Noor's heart raced in his chest, a strange heat building inside him. There was something dangerous about her, something that both terrified and thrilled him.

"You look lost." Her voice was soft, but it carried a weight that made his skin crawl.

She repeated the same as many has affirmed him before. But this time it hit him harder.

Noor swallowed, his throat suddenly dry. *"I'm not lost. Just... searching."*

The woman smiled, a slow, knowing smile that made his heart skip a beat.

"We're all searching for something. But here..." She stepped closer, her fingers brushing lightly against his arm, sending a jolt of electricity through him. *"Here, you can find whatever you're looking for. Or maybe, something you didn't even know you wanted."*

Noor felt the heat of her touch spread through him, igniting a desire he had never known before. It was more than physical, it was a hunger, a longing to be consumed by something greater than himself. For a moment, he considered giving in, letting her take him wherever this temptation would lead.

But then, he remembered the mountain, the dream, the mirror that had shown him his true self, the reflection that was fading, as if he were slowly losing who he was.

The woman's hand slipped from his arm, her eyes narrowing slightly, as she sensed the hesitation in him. *"You don't have to be afraid. Desire is not a sin. It's part of being human."*

Noor took a step back, his breath unsteady. *"But I'm not just human."*

The woman's smile faded, replaced by a look of curiosity. She studied him for a moment, her eyes searching his face as if trying to understand something about him that even he didn't fully grasp. *"No. You're not. But you're close enough."*

With that, she turned and disappeared into the shadows, leaving Noor standing alone beneath the streetlamp, the fear of temptation still pressing down on him like a heavy cloak.

As dawn broke, Noor found himself wandering the city's outskirts, where the buildings were smaller, the streets quieter. But even here, in the stillness of the morning, temptation was never far away.

A small bakery caught his eye, the scent of freshly baked bread wafting through the air. His stomach growled, and he realized just how hungry he was, not just for food, but for all the things he had denied himself since his arrival on Earth. He hadn't realized how much he had been holding back, how much he had resisted the pull of the world.

Inside the bakery, a young woman stood behind the counter, her face lit by the warm glow of the oven. She smiled as he entered, her eyes soft and kind. *"Good morning. What can I get for you?"*

Noor hesitated. He had no money, nothing to offer in exchange for the food he so desperately craved. But the woman didn't seem to care. She saw the hunger in his eyes and handed him a loaf of bread, still warm from the oven. *"Here. It's on the house and I like to feed."*

The act of kindness startled him. It was a reminder that not all of humanity was driven by greed and desire. There was goodness here, too. But even this simple act of generosity carried its own temptation, the temptation to forget his higher purpose, to immerse himself fully in the warmth and comfort of human life.

As he ate the bread, the taste filling his mouth with an almost overwhelming sense of pleasure, Noor realized just how fragile his resolve had become. The Earth was full of temptations, physical, emotional and spiritual. And every day, he felt himself slipping further into it, losing sight of the reason he had come here.

Noor thanked the woman and as he stood up to leave. The woman came forward to accept his gratitude as a price and offered, *"And do not hesitate to comeback when you are hungry. We have enough to feed the needy. Consider this as you food bank, the bank that loves you and loves you unconditionally, except that you should be truly hungry."*

That night, as Noor lay in the quiet of a small room he had rented with no money, he felt the burden of the day pressing down on him. The temptations of the earth were powerful, seductive. They called to him in ways he hadn't anticipated, making him question everything, his purpose, his path, even his own identity.

The bed beneath him was soft, the first real comfort he had felt since arriving in this world. His muscles ached, his body felt tired, but it wasn't just physical exhaustion. There was a deeper weariness, a fatigue that came from the struggle of trying to remember why he was here, what he had promised to do. Every day, it seemed like that purpose was slipping further from his grasp, buried beneath the allure of the human experience.

He tried to close his eyes to sleep as the words of the kind woman were still smiling in his mind, *'The bank that loves you.'*

That night, as he drifted into an uneasy sleep, Noor was visited once again by dreams, dreams that whispered of the temptations he had faced, and those yet to come.

In the dream, Noor stood on a vast, golden field that stretched endlessly in every direction. The sun was low on the horizon, casting a warm, golden glow over the world. There was no wind, no movement, only the stillness of the moment. Everything felt peaceful, almost too perfect.

Ahead of him, he saw a figure. It was the woman with the fiery eyes, the same one who had spoken to him in the city, the one who had ignited something inside him that he didn't want to acknowledge. She walked toward him with slow, graceful steps, her hair flowing like liquid fire, her eyes locked on his.

As she approached, Noor felt the familiar pull. Desire. Not just for her, but for everything she represented, the freedom to live in the moment, to feel, to experience life without the weight of a greater mission. In this dream, the world was empty of conflict and pain, filled only with the promise of pleasure, of indulgence. There was no duty here, no higher calling, just the raw, unfiltered beauty of existence.

The woman smiled, her lips curving into a seductive grin as she reached out to touch his face. Her fingers were warm, soft against his skin, sending shivers down his spine. *"Why do you resist? You are human now, Noor. You feel what they feel. Desire, passion, joy. There is nothing wrong with wanting these things. It is your birthright."*

Her voice was like honey, smooth and sweet, wrapping around him like a comforting blanket. Noor wanted to believe her. He wanted to lose himself in the simplicity of her words, to let go of the heavy burden he had carried since he arrived in this world. The sole purpose.

But something deep inside him resisted.

A faint echo of his true purpose stirred in his heart, like a whisper from a distant place. The image of Naina wavered in his mind, her voice, her presence, the pull that had brought him to Earth in the first place. *"I am not just human. I have a purpose... something greater than this."*

The woman's smile faltered, but only for a moment. She stepped closer, her body inches from his, her breath warm against his cheek. *"Purpose?"* she murmured. *"Isn't this purpose enough? To live, to feel, to experience all that this world has to offer. You're wasting your time chasing shadows. Naina is gone. She's lost. You can't save her."*

Noor's heart clenched at her words. Deep down, he knew that Naina was still out there somewhere, waiting for him. But the woman's words struck his deepest fear that his journey was meaningless, that no matter how hard he tried, he would never be able to save Naina from her fate, or himself from the darkness creeping in around him.

The woman's fingers trailed down his arm, sending waves of heat through his body, awakening every sense. For a moment, he let himself imagine what it would be like to give in, to embrace the life she offered, to forget the pain, the struggle, the endless search.

But then, as if sensing his weakness, the ground beneath them began to shift.

The golden field darkened, the sun dimmed and Noor saw the world around him for what it truly was, a fragile illusion, a mirage designed to seduce him away from his path. The woman's beauty faded, her eyes turning cold, empty. She was not what she seemed. She was temptation incarnate, a representation of everything that sought to pull him away from his true self.

With a sharp intake of breath, Noor pulled back, his heart racing. *"No. I will not be distracted."*

The woman's eyes flashed with anger, her smile twisting into a sneer. *"You can't resist forever. Sooner or later, you'll fall. They all do."*

With that, the world around him collapsed into darkness and Noor woke up with a shock, his body drenched in sweat, he felt his heart thrashing out of his chest.

The following morning, Noor felt drained. The dream had left him shaken, his resolve tested in ways he hadn't expected. The woman's words still echoed in his mind: "*Sooner or later, you'll fall.*"

Was it true? Could he resist the pull of the human experience forever? Could he remain true to his purpose, even as the world around him offered so much to tempt him away?

As he wandered the streets of the city, Noor found himself drawn to a small, humble sanctuary tucked away in a quiet corner. The stone walls were old and weathered, the steps leading up to the entrance worn smooth by the feet of countless worshippers. It was a place of quiet reflection, a sanctuary from the noise and chaos of the world outside.

Inside, the air was cool and still, filled with the faint scent of incense. A few people knelt in prayer, their heads bowed, their hands clasped together in silent devotion. Noor felt a pull toward eternal peace.

He knelt, his heart heavy with doubt. *"I don't know if I can do this."*

His voice was barely a whisper, but in the quiet of that space, it felt like a confession, a plea for guidance. *"The world... it's so much. It pulls at me, tempts me. I feel myself slipping away. I don't know if I can stay on the path, the Right path.. I don't know if I can find her. Oh! Lord bless me with anything beautiful. "*

There was no answer, only a soft candlelight and the distant murmur of the wind outside. But in the stillness, Noor felt a small, quiet voice stir within him, a voice that was not his own, yet somehow deeply familiar. *"Remember why you came."*

The words were simple, but they cut through the noise in his mind, anchoring him to the truth he had nearly forgotten. He had come to Earth for a reason, a purpose greater than the temptations of this world. He had come to find Naina, to save her, to fulfil the promise he had made.

Noor remembered everything from his past life. With renewed determination, he rose to his feet. The temptations of Earth were powerful, yes, but they were not stronger than his will. He had faced desire, indulgence and distraction, but he had not fallen. Not yet.

The path ahead was still uncertain, but Noor knew one thing for certain, he could not give up. He would not give up. The world would continue to tempt him, to test him, but he would face each challenge as it comes. And in the end, he would find Naina, no matter the cost.

As Noor left the sanctuary, the sun was setting, casting the city in a golden glow. He walked through the streets, his steps more purposeful now, his mind clear. The city no longer felt like a place of endless temptation, it was simply another part of the human experience, filled with both beauty and danger, joy and sorrow.

He knew now that temptation was not something to fear. It was a part of life, something every human faced. The key was not to avoid it, but to understand it, to recognize it for what it was. A test, a challenge, a way to grow stronger.

Noor had been tested and though he had stumbled, he had not fallen. The temptations of Earth were powerful, but so was his resolve.

As he made his way back to the quiet outskirts of the city, Noor looked up at the sky, where the first stars were beginning to appear. Somewhere out there, Naina was waiting for him. He didn't know where, or when they would meet, but he knew that their paths would cross again. And when they did, he would be ready.

Chapter 7
The Meeting

On the rain-soaked earth, Noor wandered the narrow, dimly lit streets of the city's outskirts. His footsteps echoed in the silence of the early evening, his mind occupied by an ever-growing sense of urgency. The city had shown him its temptations, its indulgences, and its darkness, but nothing had prepared him for this moment, this meeting he had longed for yet dreaded.

He had come here for her, Naina. Every step he had taken, every trial he had endured, had been to find her.

But now, as he stood on the cusp of finally meeting the soul he had been drawn to since the beginning, fear gripped his heart. What would she be like? Would she remember him,? as he remembered her in his dreams. Would she know, deep down, that they were connected?

But as he made his way through the twisting alleys, a growing fear began to settle over him. Something was wrong. This was not the grand reunion he had imagined, not the triumphant moment he had hoped for. There was no light here, no joy, only a cold, suffocating darkness that hung in the air like a storm wanting to break.

He rounded a corner and came to a stop in front of a small, rundown building. The paint on the walls was peeling, the windows dirty and cracked. A faint light glowed from inside, casting long, distorted shadows on the street. His heart sank in his chest, a mixture of anticipation and anxiety.

Noor stood there for a moment, rooted to the spot, his breath coming in shallow gasps. He didn't know why, but something about this place felt wrong, like a trap closing in around him. He wanted to turn back, to walk away, but he couldn't. He had come too far. He had to see her.

With a deep breath, he pushed open the door and stepped inside.

The interior of the building was dimly lit, the air filled with the smell of stale smoke and cheap perfume. The walls were adorned with faded, once-bright wallpaper, now peeling at the edges. The faint sound of laughter and muffled voices drifted from the back of the room, but Noor barely noticed. His eyes were fixed on the figure standing in the far corner, her back turned to him.

It was her. Naina.

This was her place. But he wasn't ready for the meeting at all when the Angel told him about the path to Naina. Noor was heartbroken to find Naina here working as a provider, a courtesan. The reality that never existed in his imagination. And here he is, right in front of where he always wanted to be. The entire purpose of his human existence.

Her hair, dark and tangled, fell down her back in loose waves, and her figure was slender, almost frail. She wore a simple dress, torn at the edge, her bare feet barely making a sound as she moved.

But something was wrong. This wasn't the Naina he had seen in his dreams, the ethereal soul that had drawn him to her in the land of spirits. This was someone else, someone broken, lost. She moved with a heaviness, a weariness that weighed down her every step.

Noor felt a sharp pain in his chest, as though the very air had been sucked out of the room. His mind raced, trying to reconcile the image of the radiant soul he had known with the broken woman standing before him.

He took a step forward, his voice barely above a whisper. *"Naina...?"*

She froze at the sound of his voice, her shoulders stiffening. Slowly, she turned to face him, her eyes meeting his for the first time. Noor's heart sank.

Her eyes, once filled with curiosity and light in his dreams were now dull, lifeless. There was a shadow behind them, a darkness that he couldn't ignore. Her face, though beautiful, was gaunt, etched with lines of weariness and sorrow. She looked at him with a mixture of suspicion and indifference, as if she didn't recognize him at all.

"Who are you?." Her voice was cold, detached, like a barrier between them. Noor felt the weight of her words, the distance between them growing with every second. He had expected something different, he had hoped that the moment they saw each other, something would click, some forgotten connection would spark life.

But there was nothing.

He swallowed, his throat tight. He didn't know what to say, how to explain. How could he tell her that they had met before, not in this world, but in a place beyond it? How could he tell her that their souls were intertwined, that he had been sent here to find her, to save her?

But he tried. *"My name is Noor. I've been... searching for you."*

Her expression didn't change. If anything, her gaze grew colder. *"Searching..? for me ? ... but why ?"*

He again tried to remind the connect a little more, but his words weren't helping him.*" To save you."*

"I don't need saving. I am sure of at least this", she moved away slightly with a broken smile.

Noor took a step closer, his heart aching. She was right there, but she felt so far away. He could see the pain in her eyes, the way she had built walls around herself, but he didn't know how to reach her. The connection he had felt so strongly in the land of souls was absent now, replaced by a deep, impenetrable distance. *"You don't remember me, do you?"*

Naina shook her head, a bitter smile tugging at the corners of her lips. *"No. And I don't care to. Whoever you are, whatever you think you know about me, it doesn't matter. This is my life now and I hope you know what yours is."*

She gestured around the room, her eyes filled with something cold, almost resigned. *"This is all there is. This is all I have."*

Noor felt more sadness as this was not the destiny he had imagined. He had spent so long searching for her, believing that their meeting would be the key to everything, his purpose, his salvation. But now, standing in front of her, he realized how much he had underestimated the cruelty of the world. *"It doesn't have to be like this,"* he said, his voice trembling. *"You don't have to stay here. You don't have to live like this."*

Naina's laugh was sharp, almost mocking. *"You think you can change things? You think you can save me? I don't need saving. This is my life, my choice. I chose to be here."*

Noor felt helpless, the words slipping through his fingers like sand. How could he reach her? How could he make her see that this wasn't who she was, that she was more than the broken woman standing before him?

"I don't believe that. I don't believe that this is who you are." His voice echoed.

For a moment, something flickered in Naina's eyes, a spark of recognition, of vulnerability. But just as quickly, it was gone, replaced by a cold mask of indifference. *"You don't know me. Just leave"*

Noor stood there, feeling the weight of her words press down on him like a physical force. She was right.

He didn't know this version of her. The Naina he had seen in his dreams, the soul that had drawn him to her, was not the woman standing in front of him now.

This Naina was hardened, her spirit crushed by the weight of the world. The light that had once defined her was gone, replaced by a darkness that Noor couldn't reach. She had built walls around herself, walls that he didn't know how to break down.

But despite the pain, despite the overwhelming sense of failure, Noor couldn't turn away. He had been sent here for a reason. He had come to find her, to save her, and he couldn't abandon her now, not when she needed him the most, even if she didn't know it. *"I'm not leaving,"* he said quietly, his voice steady. *"I'm here for you, whether you want me to be or not."*

Naina's expression softened, just for a moment, before she turned away. *""And what do you know about me, Noor? What do you think I am, huh? Some broken doll you can fix. You don't understand what it's like to have nothing. To be no one! You're wasting your time."*

Noor didn't respond. He didn't have the words. But he wasn't going to leave. Not now, not ever.

He tried softly, to break. *"Okay Naina, tell me, why are you doing this? I can't believe that someone as brave as you would willingly choose this... this life. Is this really what you want?"*

Naina turned to look at him, her voice calm but with a hint of defiance. *" Want? Noor, do you think anyone wants this? Do you think little girls dream of growing up to live like this? No. But life isn't about what you want. It's about what you have to do to survive, to achieve your dreams.* Naina laughed bitterly and continued, *"Convince me? Noor, you don't know what you're talking about. Everyone I know does this, in some form or another. They told me it's easy money. They told me men will pay for anything. And you know what? They were right."*

Noor was hoping for this conversation to start and this happened. *"But there are other ways. There must be. This... this isn't you, Naina. You're so much more than this. You're letting the people around you convince you that this is normal, that this is your choice. They influence you. This choice is not yours, it's your friends and your surroundings If the little girl didn't dream of growing up like this, then how did she dream of those goals that will make her walk through this path. Your values aren't aligned with your goals. This is not your choice. Don't believe it."*

"Don't you dare preach to me, Noor! Do you have any idea what it's like to be trapped in a world that only sees you as an object?" Naina exploded. *"To be told by your friends, by your family, by society that this is all you're good for. That this is survival?"*

Noor shook his head, his voice firm, *"Then why keep doing it? If it feels so wrong, if it's not who you are, why let them control you? Walk away from this, Naina. It's not too late."*

"Walk away? And go where, Noor? To what? Why?," her voice raised slightly, tinged with frustration and pain. *"The world doesn't care about girls like me. You think it's the men who pay me who are the problem? They're not the only sinners. It's everyone who turns a blind eye and lets this happen."*

"But you don't have to stay here either, Naina," he Leaned forward, his voice gentle but insistent. *You're not a sinner, Naina. You're better than this. You're—"*

"I'm not a sinner? Noor, I'm a sin eater." She cut him off, her eyes glistening but her tone resolute. *"Do you know what that means? It means I take in all their filth, all their guilt, all their shame, and I carry it so they can feel clean. They come to me with their money and their lies, and I let them pretend that what they're doing is normal. And you know what? They leave happy, but I don't. I'm left with it all. Every. Single. Time."*

Noor Struggled to find the right words, his voice choked with emotions, *"That... that sounds unbearable. You shouldn't have to bear it. You deserve better, Naina. You deserve someone to lift you out of this, not leave you drowning in it. "*

"Better? Noor, I don't even know what 'better' looks like anymore." She turned away, her voice was soft and almost broken. *All I know is this: I don't feel like a person. I'm just a mirror for their sins. I can't change what they see in me. I can't escape it. Do you know what it feels like, Noor? To feel your soul rot a little more every day? To look in the mirror and see someone you don't even recognize anymore? I feel dead inside. And you're standing here, asking me to believe in some... fantasy of escape? It's not that simple."*

Noor placed a hand gently on her shoulder, his voice steady and filled with determination. *"Maybe it's not simple, Naina. But staying in this hell isn't simple either, is it? Every day you keep going, you're letting them win. Letting them strip away the real you. But you're not dead inside, Naina. You're not beyond lost. I can see it in your eyes, there's still fight left in you. You just have to want more for yourself."*

Noor noticed slight change in Naina, he was stills struggling to understand if he is getting the right words. *"You might not see it now, but you can escape it, Naina. And you won't have to do it alone. I'm here. I'll help you find a way out. You're not just a mirror for their sins. You're a person, Naina. And you deserve to feel like one again."*

"Noor... I wish I could believe that. Yes I really do" She closed her eyes, her defenses cracking slightly as she whispered, *"but it's so hard when the world only ever sees you as one thing."*

"Then let me help you change what the world sees. Let *me remind you. Let me show you what it feels like to be free, to be whole. You don't have to do this alone. I'll stand by you, no matter how long it takes, no matter how hard it is. But you have to take the first step, Naina. You have to want it. One step at a time. Please, Naina. You're not alone in this."* His voice was firm yet filled with compassion.

Naina didn't respond immediately, but her silence spoke. After a very a long time, a light of hope stirs in her eyes. Noor's words echoed in her mind as she contemplated a life beyond the shadows she's known. It won't be easy, but maybe, just maybe, there's a path forward.

Her body was shaking as she broke down, tears spilled uncontrollably. She clutched her arms, her voice barely audible only to her, *"I don't know if I can... but I want to try."*

As the evening stretched on, the silence between them grew warmer with unspoken words. Noor stayed by her side, though Naina made no effort to engage with him. She retreated into herself, her walls firmly in place, while Noor wrestled with the thought of his failure.

But as the night grew darker, a quiet resolve settled over him.

He hadn't come this far to give up. He hadn't fought the temptations of Earth, the pull of desire, just to walk away now. There was still hope, still a chance to reach her, to break through the barriers she had built.

As he prepared to leave, Noor glanced back at Naina one last time, his heart heavy with the burden of everything unsaid. *"I'll come back for you."*

Naina didn't respond. She didn't look at him. But Noor saw the way her hands trembled, the way she gave him hope again.

Chapter 8
The Ultimate Sacrifice

Noor had never felt more helpless.

Days had passed since his first meeting with Naina, but in those days, nothing had changed. He had stayed by her side, unwilling to leave, hoping that something, anything, would break through the walls she had built around herself. But Naina remained distant, her soul locked away, buried beneath layers of bitterness and resignation. She continued her life as if he weren't there, going through the motions with a strange dctachment.

He had seen her at her lowest, watching as she numbed herself with alcohol, as she took clients, her eyes vacant, her spirit shattered. It tore his heart to witness her suffering, knowing that the light he had once felt in her was now almost extinguished.

Noor had always believed that love could save her. He had clung to that belief, even as the world around him tested him, even as he faced the temptations of Earth. But now, as he sat alone in the dimly lit room, watching her sleep restlessly on the bed, he realized the cruel truth that had been bothering him for days.

Sometimes, love wasn't enough.

The realization hit him like a blow, his chest tightened with a pain so sharp it left him breathless. He had been sent to Earth for this, for her. He had come here to save her soul, to guide her back to the light. But now, as he watched her toss and turn in her sleep, her face twisted in a grimace of pain even in unconsciousness, he understood the depth of his failure.

She was slipping away, and there was nothing he could do to stop it.

The Angel appeared to him that night, just as it had so many times before, its presence both comforting and foreboding. Noor sat in silence, his head bowed, as the Angel's voice filled the room, soft and sorrowful. *"You've done all you can, Noor."*

Noor clenched his fists, his jaw tight. *"It's not enough. I haven't saved her. I haven't changed anything."*

The Angel's light dimmed slightly, as if sharing in his grief. *"Her path was written long before you came to Earth. Some souls are destined to fall. It is not your fault."*

Noor shook his head, tears stung his eyes. *"But I love her. I can't just watch her destroy herself. There has to be something more I can do."*

The Angel was silent for a moment, and when it spoke again, its voice was filled with a gravity that chilled Noor to the bone. *"There is one final way."*

Noor looked up, his heart racing.

"But it will cost you everything." The Angel paused.

Noor listened as the Angel explained what must be done. The words rang in his ears like a death sentence, each one sinking deeper into his heart, filling him with a cold, paralyzing horror.

The Angel continued *"When a soul has committed sins too great to be redeemed, the only way to save them is through a transfer. Their sins must be taken from them, absorbed by another soul who is willing for the ultimate sacrifice."*

Noor's breath caught in his throat. He couldn't process any more when the Angel said. *"If you take Naina's sins upon yourself, you will save her from damnation. On the Day of*

Judgment, she will be free. But you... you will carry the weight of her sins, Noor. They will become your own. And when your time comes, you will face the consequences."

The Angel's voice softened, filled with an almost unbearable sadness. *"You will lose your place in heaven. You will be condemned."*

The words struck Noor like a physical blow, knocking the air from his lungs. Condemned. The idea of eternal suffering, of losing everything, felt like a cold, dark nightmare pressing down on his soul.

But then he looked at Naina, lying on the bed, her face pale and troubled even in sleep. She had suffered so much already and there was no guarantee that her suffering would end when her life did. She would be judged for her actions, for the darkness that had consumed her, and without intervention, she would be condemned to an eternity of torment.

Noor's heart ached with the weight of his love for her. He had come here to save her soul, and now he was faced with the ultimate test of that love. *"If I take her sins, will she be saved?"*

The Angel's light flickered, brighter for a moment. *"Yes. But you will be lost."*

Noor's heart raced, a whirlwind of emotions threatening to tear him apart. Could he do it? Could he sacrifice everything, his salvation, his soul, for her? He had believed that love was the most powerful force in the universe, but was his love for Naina strong enough to face eternal damnation?

He didn't know. But what he did know was that he couldn't live by himself if he didn't try.

The room was quiet, except for the soft sound of Naina's breathing. Noor stood by her bedside, his heart burdened with the decision he was about to make. His gaze lingered on her face, memorizing every detail, the curve of her lips, the faint lines of worry on her skin, the way her dark hair spilled across the pillow.

He reached out, his hand trembling and gently brushed a strand of hair away from her face. She stirred slightly, but did not wake.

Noor swallowed hard, his throat tight. He had made his decision. *"I'll do it."*

The Angel appeared beside him, its presence filling the room with a soft, ethereal glow. Noor didn't look at it, his eyes fixed on Naina as the Angel's words washed over him. *"Once this is done, there is no going back. You will carry her sins, Noor. You will lose everything."*

Noor's hand shook as he touched Naina's shoulder, his heart aching with love and sorrow. He had dreamed of this moment, of finding her, of saving her. But he had never imagined it would come to this. *"I know and I am ready."*

The Angel's light dimmed and for a moment, the room was filled with a deep, profound silence. Noor felt the burden of his choice press down on him, a crushing force that threatened to tear him apart.

And then, without warning, the air in the room shifted. It was subtle at first, a faint ripple, like the gentle stir of wind in a quiet field. But as the seconds passed, the sensation grew stronger, more intense, until it felt like the very fabric of reality was unravelling around him.

Noor gasped as a surge of energy rushed through him, filling him with a terrible, overwhelming heat. His vision blurred, his body trembling as the weight of Naina's sins began to settle upon him, dark, heavy, suffocating.

It was unbearable.

He could feel it, the greed, the lust, the anger, the despair, every sin she had ever committed, every dark thought, every cruel action, pressing down on him, crushing him beneath their weight. His mind screamed in agony, his soul buckling under the strain.

But even as the darkness consumed him, Noor held on to one thought, one hope of light in the overwhelming void.

He was saving her.

The moment passed and when Noor opened his eyes, the room was still.

He was on his knees beside Naina's bed, his body trembling, his chest struggling for breath. The weight of her sins clung to him like a cloak of darkness, but in the midst of it all, there was a strange, bittersweet peace.

Naina stirred beside him, her eyes fluttering open.

For the first time since they had met, her eyes were clear, no longer clouded by pain or bitterness. She blinked, her gaze softened as she looked at him, confused. *"Noor...? What happened?"*

Noor managed a weak smile, his heart swelling with relief. She was free. *"You're safe now. You're... free."*

Tears filled Naina's eyes as she sat up, her hand reaching out to touch his face. There was a softness in her touch, a gentleness that he had never felt from her before. *"I don't understand. What are you saying? Safe? Free? From.... what ? "*

Noor swallowed, his throat tight with emotion. *"It doesn't matter. You're going to be okay."*

Naina shook her head, tears spilling down her cheeks. *"But you... what about you?"*

Her voice was soft, filled with a raw vulnerability that Noor had never heard before. She looked at him with confusion, a dawning realization beginning to settle in her eyes, as though she sensed that something had changed. Something had been taken from her and yet, she didn't fully understand what he had done.

Noor smiled weakly, his heart aching with the weight of the sacrifice he had made, but there was a strange sense of peace within him now, knowing that she was free. He had done what he had come to do, even though the cost was far greater than he had ever imagined.

"Don't worry about me, Naina. I am at peace. I am peace." His voice was barely a whisper, strained from the immense pressure of the sins he now carried. He could feel them, heavy inside him like an unbearable weight pulling him down, but he pushed that aside for now. For this brief moment, all he could focus on was her. The way her eyes no longer reflected the darkness he had once seen in them. The way her soul seemed lighter, unburdened.

Naina shook her head, her hands trembling as she reached out and gripped his arms tightly, as if she were afraid he might disappear before her eyes.

"No... no, this isn't right. You look...." She trailed off, her gaze searching his face, and what she saw there seemed to shake her to the core.

Noor could feel his energy waning, his body weak from the sheer strain of taking on her sins. But he forced himself to remain upright, to be strong, for her sake. *"You're free now, Naina. You can live without the weight of the past. You can find your way back to the light."*

Tears streamed down her face as she shook her head again, her voice breaking. *"But what about you? What have you done? Why... why do you look like this? What did you do for me?"*

Noor's heart clenched painfully, but he held her gaze, wanting her to understand without telling her the full truth. He didn't want her to carry the burden of his choice. It wasn't something she should have to live with, knowing what he had sacrificed for her. He had made this decision willingly, and he didn't regret it. *"I did what I came here to do. To save you, to fulfill my purpose."*

Her grip on his arms tightened, and her eyes widened in fear, as if she suddenly realized what had been lost. *"No... I don't want this. I don't want you to give up everything for me!"*

Her voice was raw, desperate, but Noor gently shook his head, placing his hands over hers, his touch soft and reassuring. *"It's already done."*

Naina's breath caught in her throat and she collapsed into his arms, sobbing uncontrollably. Noor held her close, his heart breaking for her pain, but he knew it was the only way. She was safe now. She would have a chance to start over, to live a life unburdened by the sins that had once weighed her down. He could already feel the lightness in her, the way her soul had been freed from the darkness that had once consumed her.

For a long time, they sat there in silence, Naina weeping softly into his chest as he stroked her hair, comforting her in the only way he could. The heaviness in his own soul grew with each passing moment, but he didn't let it show. This moment wasn't about him. It was about her.

As the hours passed, the room grew quieter, with the aftermath of Noor's decision. Naina had fallen into an exhausted sleep in his arms, her body finally at peace after so many years of torment. Noor, too, felt the exhaustion weighing down on him, but there was no sleep for him tonight. His mind was too full, his heart too heavy with the knowledge of what lay ahead.

And then, out of the quiet, the Angel appeared once more.

Its presence was different this time, softer, more muted, as if even the Angel could sense the finality of what had transpired. Its light was dim, barely casting a shadow on the walls and its voice, when it spoke, was filled with sorrow. *"It is done, Noor. You have taken her burden upon yourself."*

Noor nodded, unable to find the strength to respond. He could feel the weight of Naina's sins pressing down on him, a constant, crushing force that drained him of his energy, his hope. But despite that, he felt a strange sense of peace. He had done what he was meant to do.

The Angel continued, *"You understand what this means."*

Noor's throat tightened, but he nodded again. *"I do."*

The Angel's form sparkled, its light growing dimmer. *"You will no longer have a place in the heavens. Your soul has been condemned by the sins you now carry. But Naina... she will be saved."*

There was a brief moment of silence, a pause in which Noor allowed himself to reflect on the enormity of the sacrifice he had made. He had known it would be this way, from the moment the Angel had told him the truth. He had known the price would be steep, but now, as the reality of it settled into his bones, he felt the weight of it in a way he hadn't anticipated.

He had given up everything, his place in eternal peace, his chance at salvation, for her.

But as he looked down at Naina, sleeping peacefully in his arms, he knew he would do it all over again if he had to. Naina, true love, was worth that price. *"What happens now?"* he asked quietly.

The Angel's form shimmered, its light softening as it spoke. *"You will remain here, for a time. The judgment of your soul will come later. But know this, Noor, you have fulfilled your purpose, even if the cost was great."*

Noor closed his eyes, his chest tightening with a mixture of grief and acceptance. There was no going back now. His fate was sealed. But there was a strange sense of closure in that knowledge. He had made his choice, and he would live with the consequences.

She was safe. That was all that mattered.

Just as the Angel was about to disappear completely, it paused, turning its gaze back to Noor with a flicker of something unreadable in its expression. *"There is something you should know, Noor. A truth about your journey that you have not yet realized."*

Noor frowned, his heart skipping a beat as he looked up at the Angel, a sense of foreboding creeping into his chest. *"What is it?"*

The Angel's light dimmed further, its voice barely a whisper as it spoke the words that would change everything. *"It was not Naina who called to you in the land of souls. It was you who reached out to her. You were the one who first felt desire, who disrupted the order of things."*

Noor's eyes widened in shock, his mind reeling from the revelation. *"What are you saying?"*

The Angel's gaze was steady, its voice filled with an odd mixture of sorrow and understanding. *"You were destined for this from the beginning. It was your own sin, your own desire, which set this path in motion. And now, you have fulfilled that destiny. It was your soul that was destined to fall, not Naina's."*

The words hit Noor like a blow, the weight of the truth settling heavily on his shoulders. All this time, he had believed that he was saving Naina, that he was the one chosen to guide her back to the light. But now he understood the full scope of what had happened.

He had been the cause of her fall. His own soul, his own desire for her, had led them both down this path. And in the end, it was only through his sacrifice that he could redeem them both.

A deep, aching sadness filled Noor's chest as he looked down at Naina one last time. She had been saved, yes. But the price had been his own soul.

As the dawn began to break, casting soft, golden light through the cracks in the walls, Noor sat in silence, his heart heavy with the weight of his fate. Naina would wake soon, free from the darkness that had once consumed her, but he would not be there when she did.

Even in the face of that inevitable doom, Noor felt no regret. He had loved her and in the end, that love had saved her. That was all that mattered.

Chapter 9
The Wait

"I await nothing. I seek nothing. I am now truly free."

Noor stood in the vast emptiness, where time seemed to stretch on without end. The world around him was quiet, devoid of the vibrant colors and sensations that had defined his journey on Earth. It was neither day nor night here, only an endless grey expanse, suspended in a space between existence and oblivion. He was alone, yet he felt the presence of the universe all around him, pressing down like an invisible weight.

He was waiting.

For what, he didn't know. His soul was in limbo, caught between the finality of his sacrifice and the unknown judgment that awaited him. The sins he had taken upon himself, the sins that had once belonged to Naina, were still with him, heavy and suffocating, but there was also something else. A light of hope, like a candle burning faintly in the darkness. It was the only thing that kept him anchored in this strange, endless place.

In the stillness, Noor found himself reflecting on everything that had brought him here. His journey, his choices, his love for Naina, it all seemed so distant now, like memories from another life. Yet, they were still with him, stitched into his soul like scars that would never fade.

Time was a concept that had lost all meaning in this place. Noor wasn't sure how long he had been here, days, years, centuries? The passage of time felt like an illusion. There were no stars, no sunrises or sunsets to mark the beginning or end of anything. Only the silence.

At first, the waiting had been agonizing. The uncertainty, the fear of what was to come, it concerned him like a living thing. He had expected judgment to come swiftly, for the sins he carried to drag him down into the abyss without hesitation. But instead, there was only this endless waiting, this quiet, suspended moment where nothing moved, where nothing changed.

He had once thought that he would be afraid when this moment came. Afraid of what awaited him after death, afraid of the price he would pay for the sins he had taken on. But now, as he stood in this infinite space, he realized that the fear has melted, replaced by something else. A quiet resignation. A calm acceptance of whatever fate had in store for him.

This waiting, this silence, it felt like a kind of penance. A final reflection before the reckoning.

As he waited, Noor's mind again wandered back to the moments that had shaped his journey, the decisions that had led him to this point. He thought of Naina, of her broken spirit, her haunted eyes and the life she had lived before he found her. He thought of the pain she had carried, the darkness that had consumed her soul and the moment he had chosen to bear that burden for her.

It had all started so long ago, in a place beyond time, in the land of souls where everything had been peaceful and still. He had been content then, unburdened by the weight of human desires, untouched by the pull of temptation. But then he had felt it, the spark of something that had drawn him to Naina, the inexplicable connection that had changed the course of his existence.

He had believed, with all his heart, that he could save her. That his love would be enough to guide her back to the light. But now, standing here in the waiting, Noor wondered if it had ever been about saving her at all. Perhaps it had always been about him, about his own soul, his own destiny. Perhaps Naina had simply been the mirror that reflected the truth of who he was.

He whispered to himself. *"Was it always meant to be this way?"*

His voice, though soft, echoed in the vast emptiness around him, as if the universe itself was listening. There was no answer, only the silence that stretched on and on, wrapping around him like a shroud.

In the quiet, Noor also found himself reflecting on the moments of doubt and weakness he had experienced. He thought of the temptations that had nearly consumed him, the woman with the fiery eyes, the allure of living a life without the responsibility of destiny pressing down on him. There had been moments, brief but potent, when he had considered abandoning his path, giving in to the temptations of the world.

But he hadn't. Even in his weakest moments, he had held on to the belief that his love for Naina could overcome the darkness. And in the end, it had, though not in the way he had expected.

He had saved her, but at what cost? He had lost his own soul in the process, condemned himself to an eternity of waiting, of uncertainty, of judgment.

A part of him wondered if it had all been worth it.

But as soon as the thought entered his mind, he dismissed it. Of course, it had been worth it. Naina was free. She had been given a second chance in life, a chance to find happiness, to walk in the light without the sins of her past dragging her down.

He had done what he had come to do.

"I don't regret it." . The words were quiet, but in the silence, they sounded like a declaration, a final statement of truth. He had no regrets. Even if the judgment that awaited him was harsh, even

if he was cast into eternal darkness, he would not regret what he had done for her.

As the waiting stretched on, Noor found himself contemplating the nature of destiny. Had everything that had happened been written long before he had made his choices? Or had his decisions, his love and his sacrifice shaped the course of his fate?

The Angel had once told him that some souls were destined to fall, that Naina's path had been set long before she was born into the world. But Noor had refused to accept that. He had believed that he could change her fate, that love could rewrite the story of her soul.

And in the end had he changed something? But perhaps it hadn't been her destiny he had altered. Maybe it had been his own.

Was it destiny that had led him to take on her sins, or had it been his own choice? Had the universe written this ending for him long ago, or had he carved it out himself, with his love and his sacrifice?

These were questions without answers and Noor knew he might never truly understand the forces that had shaped his journey. But as he waited, he found comfort in the idea that, whether written by destiny or forged by his own hand, he had fulfilled the purpose he had set out to accomplish.

He had thought, for a long time, that his fate was sealed. That his soul was condemned to eternal damnation for the sins he had taken on. But as the waiting stretched on, he began to wonder if there was still a chance, if perhaps, in some small way, his sacrifice had not only saved Naina but had also opened a door for him.

The Angel's final words echoed in his mind. *"You have fulfilled your purpose, even if the cost was great."*

Had there been something in the Angel's voice that hinted at redemption? Noor wasn't sure. But he clung to that hope, that small, fragile belief that perhaps, just perhaps, his sacrifice had been enough. Enough to save Naina. Enough to save himself.

Just as Noor's thoughts began to drift into uncertainty once more, something changed.

A faint glow appeared on the horizon, soft and distant, but unmistakable. It was a light, growing steadily brighter as it approached, cutting through the endless grey expanse that had surrounded him for what felt like an eternity.

Noor's heart leapt in his chest. The waiting was over.

He watched, his breath, as the light drew closer. It was warm, golden and filled with a sense of peace that washed over him like a soothing wave. As it enveloped him, Noor felt the burden of the sins begin to lift, ever so slightly. The darkness that had once consumed him began to fade, replaced by the gentle glow of the approaching light.

And then, out of the light, a figure emerged.

It was Naina.

Her soul glowed with the same golden light that surrounded her, her eyes filled with warmth and love. She smiled softly as she approached him and Noor felt his heart swell with emotion.

"The wait is over, Noor." Her voice was gentle, filled with a quiet strength that calmed the storm inside him.

"Naina... how are you here?" Noor was more concerned about knowing her.

Naina stepped closer, her hand reaching out to touch his. *"You saved me. And now, I'm here to bring you back."*

Noor couldn't get what he heard. Her words, simple yet filled with so much meaning, washed over him like balm. He had expected to be lost, to be condemned, to face an eternity of suffering for the sins he had taken on. But here she was, Naina, glowing with the warmth of redemption, her presence cutting through the darkness that had surrounded him.

"But how? I took on your sins. I was supposed to...." His voice trailed off, heavy with the weight of everything he had accepted about his fate. He had believed that this waiting was the prelude to his final judgment, to eternal damnation. And yet, here she stood, her light illuminating the path that had seemed so hopeless only moments ago.

Naina's smile softened, and she took his hands in hers, her touch warm and comforting. *"You sacrificed everything for me, Noor. But love, true purpose, can never be a sin. It can never lead to destruction. What you did wasn't an act of darkness. It was an act of light, of redemption."*

Noor's heart felt coldness as her words sank in. Could it be? Could his sacrifice, which he had believed would condemn him, truly lead to salvation? He had never thought of it that way, never allowed himself to hope that love with purpose, could transcend even the darkest consequences.

Naina's gaze was steady, unwavering, as she continued. *"You took on my burden, yes. But it wasn't just my sins you carried. You carried the hope that I could be saved, and that hope has power. More power than you could ever know."*

Noor's eyes filled with emotion as he looked at her, his heart torn between disbelief and overwhelming relief. *"But the Angel... it told me I was condemned. That I'd lost my place."*

Naina shook her head, her expression full of love and understanding. *"The Angel didn't have the final say. Your sacrifice did."*

As she spoke, the golden light around her grew brighter, warmer, until it enveloped them both in its radiance. Noor felt the weight of the sins he had carried for so long begin to lift, piece by piece, until the darkness that had once threatened to consume him was no more.

For the first time in what felt like an eternity, Noor felt free. The crushing burden of the sins he had taken on, the guilt, the shame, the fear, it all melted away in the light of Naina's presence. He had spent so long believing that his sacrifice would lead to his downfall, but now, standing in this light, he understood the truth.

His love for Naina, his willingness to give up everything for her, had not been a sin. It had been the path to his own redemption. The journey, the trials, the pain, they had all led to this moment, this final revelation.

Naina smiled at him, her eyes bright with tears of joy. *"You saved me, Noor. And in doing so, you saved yourself."*

Noor's heart swelled with gratitude, with love, with the overwhelming relief of knowing that he was not lost, that his soul had not been condemned to darkness after all. He had thought, for so long, that he would never see this light again, that he would never know peace. But now, here he was, standing in the warmth of that light, his soul whole once more.

Tears filled his eyes as he looked at Naina, his voice trembling with emotion. *"I thought I had lost everything."*

Naina reached up, gently wiping the tears from his face. *"You found purpose. You found love. And it is the one thing that can never be lost."*

Noor smiled through his tears, he had found love and that love had saved them both.

The light around them continued to grow, expanding outward, filling the endless grey expanse with warmth and color. Noor could feel the space around him changing, shifting, as though the very fabric of reality was being rewritten. The waiting was over.

But this was not the end.

Naina took his hand, her grip gentle but firm and together they walked forward into the light. Noor felt a sense of peace, a calm certainty that whatever awaited them now, they would face it together. He no longer feared what was to come. The path ahead was unknown, but he knew, with Naina by his side, that it would be filled with hope and possibility.

As they stepped into the brightness, Noor's heart was filled with a profound sense of joy. He had been through so much, temptation, sacrifice, loss, but in the end, it had all led to this moment. A new beginning. A chance to live, truly live, without the weight of the past hanging over him.

Naina looked up at him, her eyes filled with love and wonder. *"We're free."*

Noor smiled, the warmth of her words wrapping around him like a blanket. They were free, free from the darkness, free from the burdens they had carried for so long. Free to walk into the light, together.

And so, hand in hand, Noor and Naina stepped forward, leaving the wait behind, ready to embrace whatever future awaited them in the light of their love.

As they disappeared into the radiant glow, the grey expanse faded away, replaced by a world of warmth and color. The pain, the suffering, the sacrifices, they were all part of a distant past now. What lay ahead was something new, something pure.

Noor felt the light filling him, not just around him, but inside him, infusing his soul with a sense of peace and fulfilment that he had never known before. There was no more fear, no more doubt. Only love and boundless, unshakable hope.

And in that love, he found the redemption he had never hoped for.

In the end, it was not the statement of the Angel, nor the weight of the sins, which had determined his fate. It had been the purpose all along, the love he had carried for Naina, the love he had given freely, without expectation or demand. That love had saved them both. Because in the light of love, no darkness could ever truly prevail.

As they moved forward, into the light, Noor knew one thing for certain, their journey was far from over.

The End

About the Author

Aslam Sheik is a Dubai based Indian writer whose stories explore the profound depths of human emotions, spirituality and purpose. With a unique ability to weave heartwarming narratives that resonate with readers, Aslam Sheik delves into themes that challenge perceptions and touch the soul.

His first novel, The Other Side of the Moon, captivated readers with its poignant tale of an unconventional love story between an autistic Indian boy and a writer, a high-spirited writer Russian woman. Praised for its emotional depth and thought-provoking narrative, the book received respect and love from its readers for its portrayal of romance that defies societal norms and expectations.

In Light upon Eyes, Aslam Sheik ventures into an ethereal realm, crafting a narrative that transcends the boundaries of life and death, blending philosophy, spirituality and the timeless nature of love. With this second book, he continues to offer readers a window into worlds where emotions take centre stage, reminding us of all the beauty and complexity of the human spirit.

You can write to him on smmaslam@gmail.com, with your feedback.